Sing-Along Holiday Stories

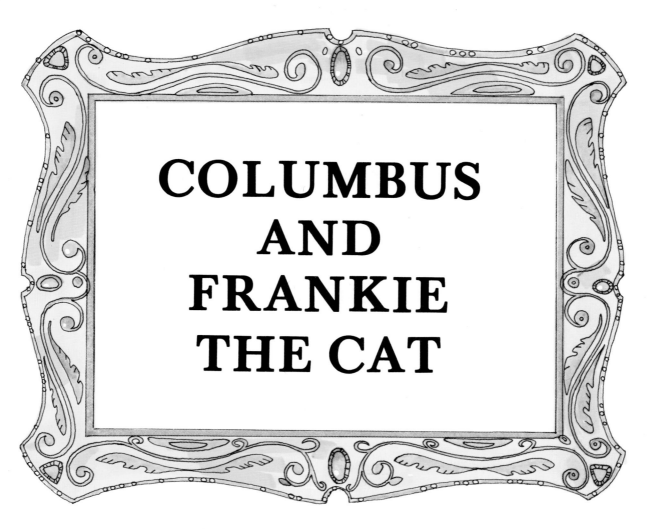

COLUMBUS AND FRANKIE THE CAT

By Carol Greene

Illustrations by Tom Dunnington

CHILDRENS PRESS®

CHICAGO

This book is for Jessica Ruhlin.

*This book can be sung
to the tune of
"My Bonnie Lies Over the Ocean"*

Library of Congress Cataloging-in-Publication Data

Greene, Carol.
  Columbus and Frankie the cat/by Carol Greene; illustrations by Tom
Dunnington.
      p.   cm.—(Sing-along holiday stories.)
  Summary: A fanciful version of the voyage of discovery made by
Christopher Columbus and his resourceful cat Frankie, to be sung to the
tune of "My Bonnie Lies Over the Ocean."
  ISBN 0-516-03462-6
  1. Children's songs—United States. 2. Columbus, Christopher—
Songs and music. 3. America—discovery and exploration—Spanish—
Songs and music. [1. Columbus, Christopher—Songs and
music. 2. America—Discovery and exploration—Spanish—Songs and
music. 3. Cats—Songs and music. 4. Songs.] I. Dunnington,
Tom, ill. II. Title. III. Series: Greene, Carol. Sing-along holiday stories.
PZ8.3.G82Cn 1989   88-33067
784.5'05—dc 19   CIP
                                                                        AC

Columbus was eating spaghetti
And making a mess on the floor,
When Frankie, his tomcat, suggested,
"Let's buy a few ships and explore."

"Yo ho! Let's go!
Let's leave all our worries behind, behind.
Yo ho! You know,
A way to the Indies we'll find."

"That sounds good to me," said Columbus.
"But we can't buy even one ship."
"You worry too much," said his kitty.
"We'll make the queen pay for our trip."

3

"Yo ho! Let's go!
Leave Queen Isabella to me, to me.
Yo ho! I know
That soon we'll be sailing the sea."

In no time he sat on the shoulder
Of Queen Isabella of Spain.
"Of course, you dear puss," she said sweetly.
"To finance your journey I deign."

"Yo ho! Oh, oh!
I've never seen travellers so bold, so bold.
Yo ho! Go, go!
And bring me back plenty of gold."

It didn't take long to get ready.
They put on their sea coats and hats.
Columbus got men and provisions,
And Frankie got cats for the rats.

"Yo ho! Let's go,
You fine feline cousins of mine, of mine.
Search high, search low,
And toss those rats into the brine."

They sailed on the Santa Maria.
The Niña and Pinta went too.
Columbus gave all of the orders.
But Frankie told *him* what to do.

"Yo ho! Fast, slow!
Look lively, me lads, to the sails, the sails.
Fast, slow! Heave ho!"
That Frankie was tougher than nails.

It seemed that they travelled forever
With nothing around them but sea.
Then one night Columbus saw firelight
Where he thought Japan ought to be.

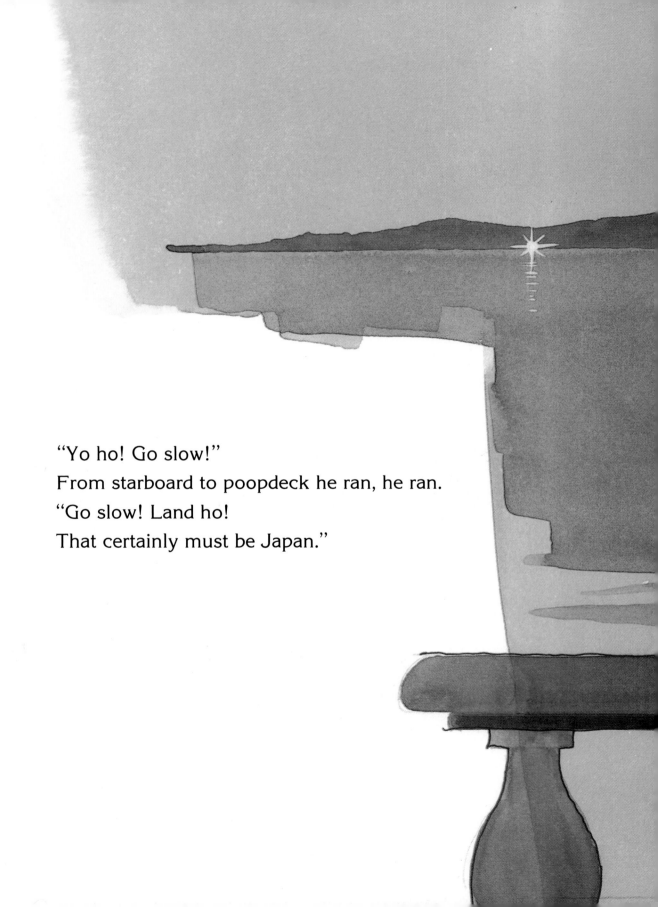

"Yo ho! Go slow!"
From starboard to poopdeck he ran, he ran.
"Go slow! Land ho!
That certainly must be Japan."

They landed the very next morning
And Frankie leaped nimbly ashore.
"This isn't Japan," he reported.
"I think you found San Salvador."

"Yo ho! Ho ho!
Stop frowning, Columbus, and smile, and smile.
Yo ho! We'll go
And chat with the natives a while."

Before long they started to barter.

Columbus got parrots galore.

He bowed and said, "Goodness! How pretty!"

But Frankie said, "Thank you. No more."

"Yo ho! Let's go.
This ship's turning into a zoo, a zoo.
Yo ho! Heave ho!
We've got more exploring to do."

From island to island they journeyed
And Frankie gave each one a name.
Columbus, however, was worried.
"This isn't the reason I came."

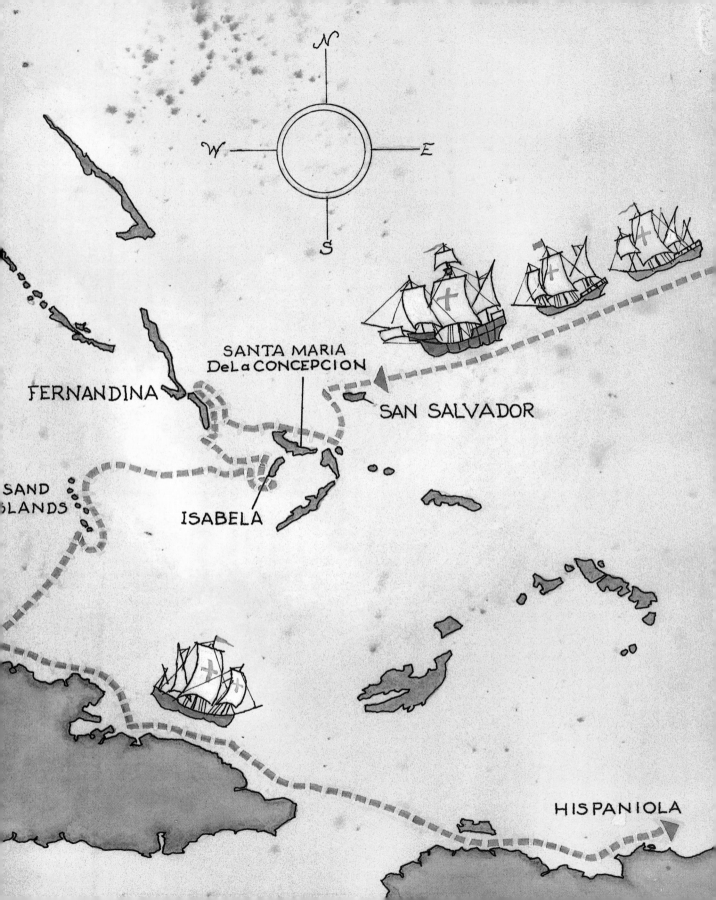

FERNANDINA

SANTA MARIA
DeLa CONCEPCION

SAN SALVADOR

ISABELA

SAND
ISLANDS

HISPANIOLA

"Yo ho! Achoo!
The queen said get plenty of gold, of gold.
Achoo! Achoo!
All I've got is birds and a cold."

The next stop was Hispaniola.
Columbus said, "*This* is Japan."
"It isn't. It isn't," said Frankie.
"You aren't making sense, my good man."

"Yo ho! Is so!"
Then suddenly they heard a clunk, a clunk.
"Is so! Oh, no!
The Santa Maria has sunk."

"It's time to go home now," said Frankie.
"We'll sail on the Niña instead.
You don't look too chipper, Columbus.
I'll run things and you go to bed."

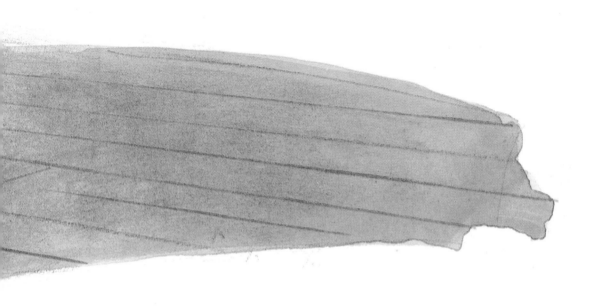

"Yo ho! Winds blow!
I'll guide us through gale and through storm, through storm.
Yo ho! You go
Drink liquids and keep yourself warm."

With Frankie as captain they made it.
The queen said, "Oh, my! What a thrill!"
"We found lots of islands," said Frankie.
Columbus said, "Frankie, be still!"

"Yo ho! I know
Japan we've discovered for you, for you.
Yo ho! That's so
And next time we'll find China too."

This isn't the way that it happened.
The history books say it's all wrong.
They have their own tale of Columbus.
But Frankie the cat wrote this song.

"Yo ho! Ho ho!
Columbus sailed over the sea, the sea.
Yo ho! *We* know
He couldn't have gone without me."

4. It didn't take long to get ready.
   They put on their sea coats and hats.
   Columbus got men and provisions,
   And Frankie got cats for the rats.

   "Yo ho! Let's go,
   You fine feline cousins of mine, of mine.
   Search high, search low,
   And toss those rats into the brine."

5. They sailed on the Santa Maria.
   The Niña and Pinta went too.
   Columbus gave all of the orders.
   But Frankie told <u>him</u> what to do.

   "Yo ho! Fast, slow!
   Look lively, me lads, to the sails, the sails.
   Fast, slow! Heave ho!"
   That Frankie was tougher than nails.

6. It seemed that they traveled forever
   With nothing around them but sea.
   Then one night Columbus saw firelight
   Where he thought Japan ought to be.

   "Yo ho! Go slow!"
   From starboard to poopdeck he ran, he ran.
   "Go slow! Land ho!
   That certainly must be Japan."

7. They landed the very next morning
   And Frankie leaped nimbly ashore.
   "This isn't Japan," he reported.
   "I think you found San Salvador."

   "Yo ho! Ho ho!
   Stop frowning, Columbus, and smile and smile.
   Yo ho! We'll go
   And chat with the natives a while."

8. Before long they started to barter.
   Columbus got parrots galore.
   He bowed and said, "Goodness! How pretty!"
   But Frankie said, "Thank you. No more."

   "Yo ho! Lets go.
   This ship's turning into a zoo, a zoo.
   Yo ho! Heave ho!
   We've got more exploring to do."

9. From island to island they journeyed
And Frankie gave each one a name.
Columbus, however, was worried.
"This isn't the reason I came."

"Yo ho! Achoo!
The queen said get plenty of gold, of gold.
Achoo! Achoo!
All I've got is birds and a cold."

10. The next stop was Hispaniola.
Columbus said, "This is Japan."
"It isn't. It isn't," said Frankie.
"You aren't making sense, my good man."

"Yo ho! Is so!"
Then suddenly they heard a clunk, a clunk.
"Is so! Oh, no!
The Santa Maria has sunk."

11. "It's time to go home now," said Frankie.
"We'll sail on the Niña instead.
You don't look too chipper, Columbus.
I'll run things and you go to bed."

"Yo ho! Winds blow!
I'll guide us through gale and through storm, through storm.
Yo ho! You go
Drink liquids and keep yourself warm."

12. With Frankie as captain they made it.
The queen said, "Oh, my! What a thrill!"
"We found lots of islands," said Frankie.
Columbus said, "Frankie, be still!"

"Yo ho! I know
Japan we've discovered for you, for you.
Yo ho! That's so
And next time we'll find China too."

13. This isn't the way that it happened.
The history books say it's all wrong.
They have their own tale of Columbus.
But Frankie the cat wrote this song.

"Yo ho! Ho ho!
Columbus sailed over the sea, the sea.
Yo ho! We know
He couldn't have gone without me."

About the Author

Carol Greene has degrees in English Literature and Musicology. She has worked in international exchange programs, as an editor, and as a teacher. She now lives in St. Louis, Missouri, and writes full time. She has published over seventy books, most of them for children. Other books in the Sing-Along series include *A Computer Went A-Courting*, *The Pilgrims Are Marching*, *The Thirteen Days of Halloween*, and *The World's Biggest Birthday Cake*.

About the Artist

Tom Dunnington divides his time between book illustration and wildlife painting. He has done many books for Childrens Press, as well as working on textbooks, and is a regular contributor to *Highlights for Children*. Tom lives in Oak Park, Illinois.